Praise for *Sold to the Highest Bidder*

"Young readers a Highest Bidder. *Eleve* beloved pony from th battles the pony ring complication arises u exquisite details, Phy young farm boy learn and friendship. Every child who yearns after the seemingly unattainable will thrill to this offering. You'll want to share this story with all the children in your life."

-- Jacqueline Guidry
Author of *The Year the Colored Sisters Came to Town*

"*In* Sold to the Highest Bidder *Phyllis Galley Westover* involves the readers so completely in the problem of eleven-year-old Jed that the result is a compelling, powerful story. Follow the journey of Jed in a summer in the 1940s as he nurses a neighbor's pony back to health. Watch how he struggles in an effort to own this pony against impossible odds. See how he learns that sometimes you have to share your love in order to keep it."

-- Suella Walsh and Lawrence Walsh
Authors of the children's novels, *Running Scared*
and *Through a Dark Tunnel*

"Jed and Tommy are real boys doing real things—learning the value of working a long day for a short day's pay, saving the money made through their own sweat labor for the one thing in life they love best, a loyal and beautiful pony named Dusty. You'll experience the sights and smells of a working farm, the tensions and excitement of an old fashioned auction, where life between the generations is anything but equal and where the triumph of goodness and love between boys and between men will make your heart stand and cheer."

-- Chalise Bourque
Author of *One Right Thing*.

Sold to the Highest Bidder

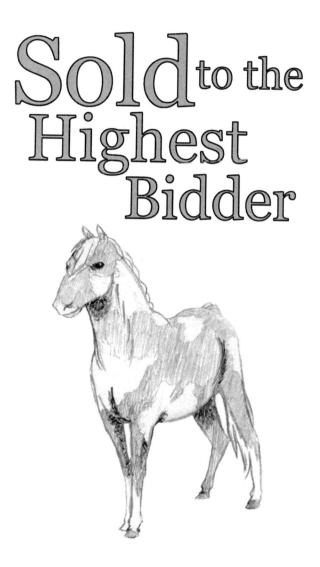

Phyllis Galley Westover

Illustrated by Jaclyn Dalbey

Sold to the Highest Bidder
Phyllis Galley Westover

This is a work of fiction. Any resemblance to persons, living or dead, or to story circumstances is purely coincidental.

pgwestover@gmail.com
phylliswestover.blogspot.com

ISBN-13: 978-1481123037
ISBN-10: 1481123033

Dedication

For every child whose best friend has four feet and a furry coat for petting; for my Grandpa Westover whose pony, "Betsy," I rode and loved for two special summers; and especially for my parents, Esther and Fred Westover, who helped me buy my horse.

Note to Parents and Teachers

Discussion questions and topics are included at the end of the book for those who would like to engage children in a conversation about the thoughts and actions that occur in the story. You will also find a list of vocabulary that may be new to some young readers.

P. G. W.

Table of Contents

Chapter 1 – Working for Pay

"Let's go there, Jed-boy!" Hank called to me. "Couple more rounds before lunch and we're done."

Done. Where was I going to get enough money? I didn't want to be done. I wanted more work.

We'd been haying for two days, Mr. Ural building the load on top of the wagon, shaking it out and packing it down to keep it from sliding. Me and Hank following with pitchforks, pitching the hay up to him.

"Hey, buck up there, Jed-boy," Hank says. "Don't look so gloomy. Best haying weather Ohio's had in two years, and for an eleven-year-old kid, you're doing great."

Hank was a good hand and nice to me. I pitched a little hay at him and tried to smile. But he didn't know what was on my mind as I scraped, scooped, and pitched, over and over to the churn of the tractor.

Then I heard Dusty. He trotted along the fence line, his head held high above the rail, whinnying. He stopped across from me and bumped the rail with his nose, jarring the fence post on either side. His white and brown patches were so slick the sun couldn't sit still on them.

"Hi, there," I told him quiet. "I see you, boy, but I can't come now. Can't you see I'm working? And it's for you I'm doing it. Did you know that? You go on and quit bothering me. I'll bring you something later."

I pitched into the hay again. He sure looked different from the first time I saw him. Mr. Ural bought him cheap at a sale last November 'cause he was run down bad—had a cold and worms. Mr. Ural's got a good eye for animals. Says he's never seen the pony yet he couldn't fix up and make a profit on. So he sized things up and bought Dusty.

I heard he'd bought a pony, so I came over the morning after the sale. Tommy must have heard, too, because he came running in the barn yelling, "Where is he, where is he, Mr. Ural!" Tommy lives one farm over. He's only eight, but we're still friends—almost as good as me and Dusty. When school's out, I don't see the town kids from my grade.

Tommy and I stood outside the stall and watched Mr. Ural work on Dusty. Dusty. The name just hit and stuck. He was dusty, and his ribs made scruffy hair rise up in grooves. His hooves were way grown out and cracked, and goo caked his nose. First thing Mr. Ural did was give him a hot mash of corn, oats, bran, and molasses and a big manger full of hay. Then he trimmed and cleaned his feet. Tommy

and I picked the burrs out of his mane and
tail, and Mr. Ural let me do the rubdowns.

Each day after school I rode my bike to Mr. Ural's to see Dusty. He got to expect me at 3:40 sharp. Soon as I leaned my bike against the barn, I'd hear him nicker.

"Hi, boy," I'd say sliding the door open. "How're you doing today? You getting rid of that cold yet? We've got lots to do together soon as you get well. When you're perky again and the weather's nice, I'm going to take you to my favorite spot in all the world—down by the creek and woods."

I ran my hand and the brush down his back and sides. "But first you gotta plump out. Sittin' on you now would be like sittin' on a washboard—and I might hurt your ribs and I sure wouldn't want to do that."

I talked to him about learning each other's ways, getting well, and about lots and lots of things we'd do afterwards. We had an understanding. He listened good and always found the carrot sticks in my pocket that I saved from my lunch. Weekends, Tommy brought him apples from his folks' orchard.

After Dusty got rid of the worms, he did fill out, and grazing with his head down in March drained his cold. His spring coat came in short and shiny. But guess I should've been talking to Mr. Ural about afterwards.

We came to the end of the field. The wagon moved toward the barn, the tractor whining in low gear. I stopped at the watering trough to splash my face then walked into the coolness of the barn to the water spigot and drank till I almost burst. Then I flopped back against a hay bale to watch. Tommy came in the side door and sat down beside me.

"Jed, how much you going to make this pay day?" He was keeping track with me.

"Near a hundred, I guess" I said, "but . . ."

"Not enough yet, is it?" For a little kid, Tommy was pretty smart with numbers.

I shook my head and Tommy tucked his chin and beat the heel of his sneaker against the dirt floor.

Mr. Ural was yelling directions on how to back the wagon up the ramp. Wonder if there's ever a time he's not bossing and changing things.

This was the last pay I'd get before the county auction. Tomorrow, most all Canton would be at the opening of the county fair. That's where Mr. Ural was taking Dusty. The wagon eased into the barn, and the tractor stopped. Mr. Ural came around the edge of the load covered with bits of hay.

"All right fellows. Let's get the business settled," he said.

He pulled out of his back pocket a brown, bent wallet. I went over to him with the others.

"Jed, I owe you for work done on the fence line and haying, if I'm correct. You did a right fair job for a kid."

"Thank you, Sir."

I took the wrinkled bills and walked out into the sun. Tommy caught up with me and we counted my pay. Eighty dollars, and that's all the money there'd be. Tommy squinted up at me against the sun, his freckles shining like Dusty's spots. "I've got twenty-five dollars, Jed. It's my allowance savings. You can have it for Dusty if I can ride him, too."

I knew he meant it. And it was real nice because he was also saving up for a pony. He'd told me that he was starting now, so by the time he was eleven, he could buy one.

"Thanks, Tommy," I told him. "Sure, if Dusty were mine, I'd let you ride, but even together we don't have six hundred dollars."

"Might help. Maybe Dusty will go for less."

I shook my head. "Mr. Ural won't sell him for less, and besides, Dusty looks too good now. He'll run up the bids."

I stuffed the money back in my pocket and said, "We're late for dinner. Better get going." Tommy took off on his bike, and I headed home.

Chapter 2 – Figuring a Way

Where was I going to get another hundred dollars before tomorrow afternoon? Every cent I'd earned for a year at the grocery store Saturdays, at the gas station Sunday afternoons, and on Mr. Ural's farm since June I'd kept in a coffee can for the day I'd have enough to buy Dusty.

I took the short cut through the field, rolling under the Urals' fence into our cornfield to walk between the rows. Every time the air blew, the leaves rattled, and I could smell them strong as I tried to figure. With this last eighty dollars, my savings still only came to five hundred—only five hundred twenty-five, counting Tommy's savings. Looking out over the wheat stubble field and squares of pasture, seemed like everything wavered in the heat.

I'd already asked Mr. Ural if he'd sell Dusty to me for less. He'd only grunted. "Didn't get him well for nothing," he said. And I knew Dusty was worth at least the six hundred Mr. Ural planned to get for him.

I climbed our back steps and shoved open the porch screen door.

"That you, Jed?" Mom called from the kitchen. "Where you been? Dad's sat down and grace's been said."

"Working," I said.

"Go wash up and come eat." She wiped her hands on her apron, and looked at me like she was sizing up the weather.

I slid into my place. Chops, mashed potatoes, sweet corn, fresh tomatoes, and muffins. Most times, I can hardly wait for my folks to start so I can begin. But nothing looked special to me that day, except the muffins. Dusty liked muffins. I'd take a couple to him later.

"Been expecting a little help with the stock this week, son," Dad said.

"If he weren't so occupied with that pony all the time," Mom said, "he might get the things done around here that ought to get done."

Dad raised his bushy eyebrows and looked at Mom over his ear of corn. Dinner ended quiet. I guess Dad knows how it is. He doesn't have to tell me about chores often. I followed him out to the barn and cleaned out the stalls real good while he worked on the truck.

Where was I going to get another hundred dollars? I put up my pitchfork and leaned on the fender watching Dad. He knew how to fix just about everything, and he was mighty particular about our Studebaker pickup.

"Dad?"

"Yes, Son?"

"I've got five hundred dollars saved to buy Dusty."

"That's a lot of work and saving."

"But Mr. Ural won't sell Dusty for less than six hundred, and he's taking him to the fair auction tomorrow."

Dad put down his wrench and squeezed my arm. "Jed, it's hard. But you know why Mr. Ural bought Dusty. He's put a lot of money into him."

"But I helped him get him well."

"I know, but it wasn't your money that bought, fed and doctored him."

"Dad, do you think . . . you might loan me a hundred so I could buy him before the auction? I could work for you instead of at the gas station and for Mr. Ural. Wouldn't take long to pay you back."

"Wish I had it to loan you, Jed, but I don't." He ran his hand down my arm and with his shoe scraped a piece of wire away. "You know I count on your help as it is. We can't afford to be hiring extra help. It's just the three of us, except for haying."

I knew. It was the same with Tommy's folks, but I had to try. The last two years were bad for farmers. My last chance was that Mr. Ural might let me give him all the money I had for Dusty and then keep on working for him until I could pay off the rest. I shaded my eyes against the afternoon sun and walked back down the path to find him.

At the top of the rise, I saw him clearing out brush with the team at the far end of the pasture.

"Afternoon, Mr. Ural," I said, stopping by his next pile. "Sure is hot, isn't it?"

He nodded and pulled the team to a stop. I watched my shoe scraping the dirt.

"Mr. Ural, I can work real hard, and I can help you this winter, too. It won't take long for me to pay you the rest—I got five hundred dollars already. I could feed the stock, clean the stalls. I could shovel the path to the barn and get the wood, and I . . . ."

Mr. Ural looked away fast and turned to the team.

"Got all the help I can use for winter. It's the money I need. Can't do it." He picked up the reins and snapped them across the team's backs. "Gettup there, Whitey! Hyaaaaaaaa, come around there, Jerry! Steady now, together! Hyaaaaaaaa!"

The team jumped, and Mr. Ural and the brush jerked along after them. I just stood there. Then I ran. I didn't know why. I just ran. At the end of the pasture, I rolled under the fence into the long grass next to the woods. I pushed my way through the high weeds, tripping over thick ones. Then I was in the shade of the trees.

I dropped down on the bank of the creek. I couldn't breathe right or quit shaking. I lay there, my face pushed into the damp leaves, listening to the quiet and my breathing. After a while I got better. I dangled my hands in the water and held them against my eyes and rolled over on my back. The trees make a roof here in my spot in the woods. The sun gets through little spaces between the leaves, making pale streaks. You can see bits of dust jumping in them. The cicadas sawed their song. Every now and then a crow called. A squirrel jiggled the branches.

My maple's a good climber. I jumped, locked my fingers around the lowest branch, and walked my feet up the trunk to where I could swing over the branch and lean against the trunk. This is my thinking tree where I come to be alone. I puzzled about Mr. Ural and what I could do. It's strange about grown-ups. Maybe it's something that grows down in them while everything else is growing up. You'd think they'd get it—that with all that living you wouldn't have to keep explaining it to them, how it is. But they don't hear it the way you say it—don't understand an animal being your friend.

There wasn't much left to think about. I wouldn't get the hundred dollars in time. The next day Dusty would be sold to the highest bidder. But I made up my mind to go to the auction anyway and bid my five hundred for all it was worth. I could do that much for Dusty.

I must have stayed a long time. The shadows of the leaves changed shapes on the ground. A squirrel chattered and stirred me out of my thinking. I swung down and started home.

Chapter 3 – Saying Good-bye

Next morning, I woke early and sneaked downstairs. Mom wasn't in the kitchen yet, so I put a muffin in each pocket and left, quiet. I wanted to see Dusty one more time before the auction and make sure he looked his best, even if he was to be sold.

The barn was cool from the night air, and even though the stock were all awake, they were still lying down. Their breathing made the barn smell even better. Dusty lay in the far corner of his stall with his legs tucked under him. He watched me. His nose wiggled like he whispered a nicker, and he got up and shook. The team and the cows watched me, too, their ears moving up and back like they wondered what I was doing there so early. But I don't mind animals looking at me. They don't try to change things.

"Hi," I said to them all.

I tried to spot the currycomb and brush on the top shelf. Thin bars of sunlight from the hayloft window shone between the ceiling planks. The flies were still asleep. They clung to the cracks between the boards, making a row of black polka dots. I stretched and ran my fingers along the whiskery grain of the top shelf until I felt the bristles of the brush. Then I jumped and knocked down the brush and currycomb next to it and went to Dusty. He

stretched his neck out and nudged my
pockets.

"Hungry? Hey, quit that! You want to
knock me over?"

I pulled a muffin out of my pocket and
held it out flat on my hand. He crumbled it
with his lips and whisked it into his mouth.

"Muffins, that's what I ought to name y . . .
Well, that's what someone ought to name
you."

I pushed back his forelock so I could see
his white star on the brown again. Then I
pushed back my hair. Mine's almost the same
brown. I set to work currying and brushing,
telling him how proud I was of him and that
he was my best friend, ever. When I was
finished, I pet him and scratched him behind
the ear a bit. Then I ran my cheek down his
muzzle and said, "Good-bye, Dusty. I won't be
seeing you anymore."

Chapter 4 – The Fair

We could hear the fair a mile from the grounds. Dad drove through the main gate and under the big sign lit up in bulbs: "Stark County Fair – 1948." I helped Mom carry the picnic fixings from the parking area to the pavilion.

Tommy's family was there early, too. He saw me and came running with a big grin. I wondered what he had to be so happy about.

"Jed, Jed! Uncle Joe's here from Chicago! He's going to give me a ride in his new Chevy! He came for the fair and is staying for my birthday!" I'd forgotten Tommy's birthday was the next weekend. He thought a lot of his uncle, and his uncle must have thought a lot of Tommy because he gave Tommy a bike for Christmas.

"Uncle Joe, come here! Uncle Joe!" Tommy went roaring back to his uncle and pulled him by the hand over to our table. My folks had met him before at Tommy's place, but I hadn't. "Uncle Joe, this is my best friend, Jed. He's going to the auction to try and buy Dusty with all his savings, and I'm saving, too, so I can buy me a pony in three years."

"Well now, you two, those are very ambitious plans. I'm proud to meet such an industrious young man," Uncle Joe said to me, "and I wish you luck at that auction."

We shook hands, and I said, "Thank you, Sir." He was being really nice, but I didn't feel very lucky.

"Uncle Joe, will you go to the auction with me?" Tommy said, grabbing his hand again. "I know where it is. I can show you."

"Why that would be my honor to accompany you," Uncle Joe said, ruffling Tommy's hair.

"You two kids have a look around the fair," Dad said. "We men are going to the stock pens and show this city slicker uncle what farm animals look like." He slapped Uncle Joe on the back and winked at Tommy, tugging his ear. Tommy tilted his head, grinning even more and showing the two empty spaces where he was waiting for his big teeth.

"Be back by noon," Mom said.

The auction wasn't until 2:00, so we wandered around those wide sawdust paths. Motors were winding up and cutting down—

everything was moving. A man with a straw hat, cane, and striped shirt was yelling to the crowd: "Step this way, please! Ladies and Gentlemen, see the one, the only fire eater and sword swallower! Step inside and see the fattest fat woman and thinnest thin man!"

"Geez," Tommy said, looking at the big posters. "Think she could really be that fat? Must take a tractor to move her."

I just shrugged and we moved on.

We watched a man spin pink cotton candy around a brown cone inside a big metal kettle. It had been a year since I'd had any. But they cost a quarter.

Then we heard squeals and a big whoosh and the clickity-clack of wheels on a track. "Come on!" Tommy said, tugging me by the hand. "It's the Wildcat!"

We followed the sounds to the rollercoaster loading platform and watched dizzy passengers stumble out of cars and down the ramp, laughing. Even I had to smile.

"Want to ride?" Tommy said, looking up at me.

"Can't. Not yet."

"Oh," Tommy said. "Maybe next year."

We followed the sound of half-pretty, half-sour organ music to the merry-go-round and watched painted wooden horses and the ones with the horn in their foreheads going up and down. Looked like they'd keep going and stay beautiful forever. Then we came to a live merry-go-round. Ponies walked around a track in the sun tethered to a pole that turned. I wondered if they ever got water and a break in the shade. Little kids sat on the ponies, kicking. The ticket man wore a suit and white shirt with one of those dude string ties. He waved me toward the gate.

"Just fifty cents a ride! Come pick your pony, kid!"

I shook my head and shoved my hands in my pockets. My fist closed around my five hundred dollars for Dusty. We headed back. It was almost noon.

Mom was unpacking the lunch basket. Tommy took off to sit with his family. He said he'd see me at the auction with his uncle. I sat on the bench and chipped a long splinter out with my thumbnail. Mom kept watching me out of the corner of her eye.

"You sure you want to go to that auction?" she asked.

I nodded without looking up.

"Jed, why you hanging on so? You're just hurting for nothing." She brushed a wisp of hair from her cheek. "Some nice farmer will get that pony. Now I mind the time when I was a girl and wanted a kitten . . ."

Then she quit. Her voice got soft and she quit. She kept wiping the top of a pickle jar like she thought it might be dirty. I fiddled with the splinter.

Farm friends gathered around the table with their baskets, laughing and talking about the exhibits and prizes. I ate the edge from a sandwich. Maybe there was a chance. I didn't see how Mr. Ural could stand to sell Dusty, either. Hadn't he seen him everyday, too— seen him get well, made Dusty's shoes at his own forge? Maybe when he saw Dusty out there, he'd call him off the floor.

I'd go. Even if someone else got him, I wanted to see who it was and tell them how to care for him. I promised to meet Mom and Dad at the car at five, and then I pushed through the crowd to find the auction.

Chapter 5 – The Auction

From the outside the building looked like a
barn, only bigger. Inside it was all different.
One side had bleachers, like at the ballpark,
and in front of the bleachers was a sawdust
ring. Behind the ring was the auctioneer's box,
tall, with a microphone in front and a gavel
resting on top. Doors on both sides of the box
went to the stalls, pens, and payment desk

behind the wall. I looked around, but I didn't see Mr. Ural. I found a seat in the center and waited for the livestock. Farm machinery was being auctioned off. Usually, I liked auctions because of the way the auctioneers talk. This time, I didn't like the sound at all, and every time the auctioneer banged his gavel at the end of a sale, I jumped a little. I tried not to listen. I squirmed around on the bench and crushed the halves of three peanut shells with my shoe.

Mr. Ural came in and sat on the front row to the right. He didn't look my way. Other farmers and families came in. Men packed their pipes. Some poked chewing tobacco in their mouths. They folded their arms across their baggy overalls and talked about reapers, a new foal, or the haying. When they couldn't talk around the tobacco juice any longer, they'd stop and spit. Women held babies on their laps and talked about new washers and damp cellars. Little kids ran up and down the bleachers, losing most of their popcorn. I half listened in because it took my mind off the auctioneer. But I kept spreading and curling my toes inside my shoes through the show of cattle, sheep, and hogs. I looked for Tommy and his uncle and saw them moving into about the only place left near the back. It was about time for the ponies.

Then this new man came in. I might not have looked up, except that the farmers quit talking. There was one of those quiet spells when you think something's going on. This new man had on a suit like Dad wears to church, only this was no church and he should have known that. He didn't find a place down front, so he came back up and pushed in a couple of rows in front of me, making people squeeze together. That's when I saw he had on a white shirt and string tie. It was the ticket man from the pony ring.

"Timed it just right for the little ones," he says too loud, poking the man next to him with his elbow.

He didn't talk like us, either, and what he said made me feel hot.

"Got a pony ride string," he says, lighting a cigarette. "You know, fifty cents a ride for a couple of turns. Darn good business. Can't lose. Not much overhead or upkeep. With all the fairs I do, you can rake it in, and you can always pick up new ponies when you need to."

All I could think was "Dusty!" But it was too late to get to him. The bleachers were jammed. People even sat on the side steps. The first pony was led in, and the rest were lined up and numbered beyond the door where the stableboy stood. I couldn't see Dusty. I stood up and tried to get Mr. Ural's attention, but he was talking and looking the other way. I sat down and tried to wait. Everything looked blurred. But I could hear okay. It had started. Two ponies not half so pretty as Dusty were auctioned off for four hundred and four fifty.

I kept watching the door to the stalls. Then I saw him, his forelock bobbing up and down behind the stableboy. I could feel my heart pounding in my head. I held on to the bench. Dusty looked good—too good. The room got louder, then quieter. Two farmers below me nodded toward Dusty, and the pony ring man crushed his cigarette and sat up.

The auctioneer's helper waved a fancy cane and made Dusty trot back and forth around the sawdust circle. Dusty jumped and shied at the cane, and I was too far away to stop the man. Mr. Ural was sitting on the front row. Why didn't he stop him? He just sat there with his arms folded. The bidding began.

"Come a, come a, come a, come a, what am I bid for this pretty little pony?" the auctioneer boomed out over the stands.

A man at the side called, "One hundred!"

"Come a, come a, come a, who'll make that one twenty-five?"

The pony ring man elbowed the man next to him again and said, "One twenty-five!"

I looked away from Dusty and came to with a jump. It was happening. They were bidding for Dusty. I dug my fingernails into the bench.

"One fifty!" yelled the auctioneer.

"One fifty!" I yelled back as loud as I could.

Several people turned around to look at me, and so did Mr. Ural. I kept looking at the auctioneer. I had to make him understand he couldn't sell Dusty—not to the pony ring man, not to any of them. Dusty was mine.

"Come a, come a, come a, come a, do I hear one seventy-five for this pony?"

"One seventy-five!" yelled the man at the side.

"Come a, come a, make that two hundred!" the auctioneer called.

"Two hundred!" said the pony ring man with two others. I couldn't make the auctioneer hear me above the men.

"Come a, come a, come a, who'll bid two twenty-five?" the auctioneer's voice was getting sharper.

"Two twenty-five!" called three voices from the back.

"Come a, come a, who'll make it two fifty?!"

"Two fifty!" I yelled with three others and the pony ring man.

The auctioneer took a big breath, "Come a, come a, come a, come a, who'll bid two seventy-five?!"

"Two seventy-five!" I yelled fast with my hands clenched at my sides before anyone else could answer. Families around were watching me.

"Mama, how come he can bid alone?" a little girl said loud.

"Hush," her mother told her.

"Come a, come a, come a, three hundred!"

"Three hundred!" said the pony ring man. He was sitting forward with his elbows on his knees.

"Who'll make that three fifty?" the auctioneer said like a dare. He was stepping up the bids.

"Three fifty!" I answered him. My voice didn't sound the same. It was higher and I couldn't yell as loud.

"Three fifty, come a, come a come a, four hundred!"

"Three seventy-five!" said the pony ring man.

"Four hundred!" I yelled before the auctioneer could call the bid. The crowd mumbled. I dug my nails deeper into the bench. People were looking first at me, then the auctioneer, then the pony ring man who lit another cigarette. I sat on the edge of the bench, holding hard to both sides.

"Who'll make that four fifty?"

"Four fifty!" said the pony ring man.

I let go of the bench and slid my hands into my pockets and around the money. The stand was still.

"Come a, come a, come a, come a, who'll bid five hundred for this fine little pony?" The auctioneer leaned way over his box.

I jumped up with the money clenched in my fists. "Five hundred, Sir!" I said as loud as I was able. I looked him right in the eye.

The auctioneer stopped and looked at me. Then he looked at Mr. Ural. Mr. Ural sat with his arms still crossed in front of him. Then he slowly shook his head.

"Mr. Ural!" I cried out. I couldn't help it. But he didn't turn around. I know he heard me because there wasn't any other sound. He sat looking straight ahead.

The auctioneer started in again. "Come a, come a, come a, do I hear five twenty-five?"

I was still standing there with the money in my fists. A low mumble went through the stand again.

"Five twenty-five!" a high voice yelled from the back. It was Tommy bidding his allowance for me. I turned around and looked at Tommy. I guess everyone in the bleachers did. And then they looked at me.

"Five fifty," said the pony ring man. He was the only one who spoke.

I sank down to the bench and pushed the money back in my pockets. I couldn't hold it in any longer. Everyone around was looking at me, and I could feel my neck and shirt getting wet.

I put my head down on my knees and my arms up over my ears. I didn't want to hear any more, and I didn't want anyone looking at me, but I couldn't have made it out. The bidding kept on. Others got back in it again. They were up to five seventy-five.

The lady behind me gave me a pat on the shoulder and her handkerchief. I looked at the ring. Dusty was still trotting around the ring with his mane and forelock jouncing. The auctioneer's helper had the lead rope short and high so Dusty had to hold his head way up and back. I shouldn't have looked. I put my head down again. The pony ring man was having it out with the man at the side. I hoped the man at the side would get Dusty. He looked like my dad on workdays. Then I felt someone wiggle in next to me. It was Tommy. "I'll sit with you, Jed," he said, and put his arm around my shoulder.

"Six hundred!" the auctioneer called.

"Six hundred!" said the man at the side.

I put my head up again. Mr. Ural said he'd sell Dusty for six hundred. Maybe he'd stop the bidding and let the man at the side buy Dusty. But no, Mr. Ural had said for not less than six hundred. The bidding kept going.

"Come a, come a, come a, six twenty-five!"

"Six twenty-five!" said the pony ring man.

"Come a, come a, six fifty!"

No one bid. I turned to look at the man at the side. He had his hands held up in front of him and was shaking his head.

"Come a, come a, come a, come a, six twenty-five, once!" The auctioneer looked around.

"Six fifty!" a new voice called. Tommy jerked around, and I looked with him. It was Tommy's uncle.

"Uncle Joe!" squealed Tommy, jumping up. Now the crowd was really watching— everyone except the pony ring man.

"Come a, Come a six seventy-five!"

"Six seventy-five," said the pony ring man.

Tommy made a high groaning noise. "The pony ring man's going to make Uncle Joe run out of money, too. It'd take two people's money to outbid him," he said, stamping on a popcorn box.

That's when I knew. I clenched the money in my pockets again. "Tommy, that's it! Let's get back to your uncle!" We squeezed by the people on the bench and ran up the aisle.

"Come a, Come a, Come a, who'll make that seven hundred?"

"Seven hundred," said Tommy's Uncle Joe, but he was frowning.

"Uncle Joe!" Tommy said, "Jed's got a plan."

"Here, Sir," I said, "take my money. Please. You can outbid him with my money, too. Please, don't let Dusty go to the pony ring man! Buy him for Tommy's birthday!" I pushed my fist-fulls of bills into his hands. It was the first time in my life I'd seen an adult look truly shocked.

But then Uncle Joe smiled. "Okay, Jed. It's a plan. This is for both you and Tommy." He pulled us down on either side of him and gave us a squeeze.

"Come a, come a, come a, seven twenty-five for this fine pony!"

"Seven twenty-five," said the pony ring man.

"Come a, come a, come a, seven fifty!"

"Seven fifty," said Uncle Joe.

"Who'll make it seven seventy-five?"

"Seven seventy-five," said the pony ring man, shaking his head.

The crowd was really into it, like they were following a boxing match.

"Come a, come a, come a eight hundred!"

"Eight hundred," said Uncle Joe.

"Come a, come a, eight fifty for this spectacular pony!"

The pony ring man threw down his cigarette and ground it out with his boot. He pushed to the aisle, and glaring at us he said loudly on his way out, "Sheesh, some people just don't appreciate a business."

"Eight hundred once! Eight hundred twice! Eight hundred three times! Sold to the highest bidder, the gentleman and two boys, for eight hundred dollars!" And he banged his gavel down hard on the box.

Then the strangest thing happened. As we made our way down to settle up out back, everybody clapped. All I remember after that was that I had my arms around Dusty's neck and he was nuzzling my pockets.

Chapter 6 – Fifty/Fifty

On nice days Tommy and I ride Dusty down to my thinking spot. We tether him to graze while we sit on our favorite limbs and talk. Dusty agrees with most everything we say. We puzzle about who Dusty belongs to, but can you really own a friend? I don't think an animal can ever truly belong to someone. The way we figure, we're guardians—like with adopted kids. Dusty must know we're all one big family, 'cause he nickers whenever he sees us coming and bumps his pink nose right against my pocket.

Tommy says Dusty is mostly mine because I worked the longest to earn the most money to buy him, and I had the idea to add my money to Uncle Joe's. But I tell him, no, that's not right. I didn't have enough money alone, and it was Tommy's bidding his allowance on top of my money and saying it would take two people's money to outbid the pony ring man that gave me the idea to give my money to Uncle Joe. And if it hadn't been for Uncle Joe jumping in the bidding, Dusty would be at the pony ring now. But, anyway, it's all settled. Uncle Joe had us sit down together with our folks, and we all agreed that the best thing was to split the cost and care of Dusty fifty/fifty. So, I got a hundred dollars back from my five hundred, Uncle Joe paid three hundred seventy-five, and Tommy paid twenty-five.

I reckon even Mr. Ural is finally happy since he got a lot more for Dusty than he'd planned on.

Sometimes Dusty sleeps over at Tommy's place and sometimes at mine. He doesn't mind, and Tommy and I think that sharing a pony is the very best present either of us ever got. We told Uncle Joe he could ride Dusty whenever he came to visit.

About the Author

Phyllis Galley Westover grew up in New York City loving animals. A cat and a dog fit in her parents' apartment, but a pony did not. So, she saved all the nickels and dimes given her for ice cream cones and all her allowance from the time she was six until she was twelve when her family moved to Alabama. Finally she was big enough to ride a horse and had a place for one. But she only had enough money for half a horse, so she bought one with a friend. And guess what? Her parents surprised her by buying the other half!

She also loved stories and to write, so many years later she went to college, earned degrees, and began to teach and write. You can read her stories in magazines and anthologies. For more information about her teaching and writing career, see her website at **PhyllisWestover.blogspot.com**.

About the Illustrator

Jaclyn Dalbey is an illustrator and filmmaker living on the roaring plains of Kansas City. She graduated from the Kansas City Art Institute in 2011 and is currently paying her rent. For more information about her work, see her website at **JaclynDalbey.blogspot.com**.

Acknowledgments

My great thanks go to reader friends and to the Kansas City Writers Group for their thoughtful suggestions on early drafts and for their fresh, sharp eyes in proofing. My thanks also to Write Brain Trust friends and Mary Schmidt for technical assistance and support that made this book possible. Special thanks to Dillon Boor for his suggestions on illustrations.

Discussion Questions and Topics
(Select according to age, maturity and experience)

Questions relating to the story:

- Have you ever wanted something so much that you couldn't think of anything else and tried every honest way possible to get it?
- How many ways did Jed try to get enough money to buy Dusty?
- Did Jed's family help? What did his parents think about his trying to buy Dusty? Did they care that Jed would likely not get Dusty? How do you know?
- What was special to Jed about the tree he went to sit in after talking to Mr. Ural? Do you have a place like that?
- Why didn't Mr. Ural allow Jed to work off the remaining dollars to buy Dusty? Was he just being mean?
- When Jed and Tommy looked around the county fair, why didn't they go on any of the rides or even buy any cotton candy?
- How did Jed feel about the pony ring and its ponies?
- What made Jed even more worried about the outcome of the auction?
- Would you have gone to an auction alone to bid for something you wanted? Why or why not?
- How did the other people at the auction feel about Jed's bidding for Dusty? How do you know?
- How did Tommy help Jed?
- What idea did Jed get from Tommy?
- Why was Tommy's Uncle Joe shocked by what Jed said and did?
- Did you ever give something away to protect someone or something you love?

- How does working together help get what you want?
- How did Uncle Joe and Tommy's and Jed's families work out the ownership of Dusty so it was fair to all?

General Discussion Topics:

- When is cooperation and good planning with other people a good idea? Can you think of examples of when you've seen this or when you think it should be tried? What are the advantages? What disadvantages may there be?
- What do you think about Jed's saying that he doesn't think "an animal can ever truly belong to someone"? Can an animal be your friend, and can you own a friend? Can you be their guardian? Is this the same for wild animals as for pets or farm animals? How should we treat and relate to animals?

The vocabulary or usage below may be new to some young readers:

Adopted	Exhibits	Manger	Rubdowns
Ambitious	Forelock	Molasses	Scruffy
Auction	Forged	Muzzle	Shied
Auctioneer	Frowning	Nicker	Spigot
Bid	Gavel	Nuzzle	Squealed
Bleachers	Graze	Outbid	Squirming
Burrs	Grooves	Pavilion	Stalls
Cigarette	Grunted	Perky	Stock pens
City slicker	Guardians	Pitchfork	Stubble
Clenched	Hooves	Plank	Studebaker
Clung	Industrious	Plump	Sword
Currycomb	Jarring	Polka dots	Tether
Doctored	Jouncing	Reapers	Tractor
Eased	Limb	Reckon	Wallet

CPSIA information can be obtained at www.ICGtesting.com
Printed in the USA
LVOW11s1636110414

381361LV00012B/487/P